THE MONSTER BED

Jeanne Willis · Susan Varley

Andersen Press · London

Never go down to the Withering Wood,
The goblins and ghoulies are up to no good.
The gnomes are all nasty, the trolls are all hairy
And even the pixies and fairies are scary.

Oh, never go down there, unless you are brave,
In case you discover the Cobbeldy Cave.
For inside that cave which is gloomy and glum
Live Dennis the monster and Dennis's mum.

Now Dennis the monster was mostly polite;
He tried very hard not to bellow and bite,
Except, I'm afraid, when the time came for bed.
"I'm frightened! I'm frightened!" the wee monster said.

"But why?" asked his mummy. "There's nothing to fear,
I've given you teddy, the light switch is here."
"The humans will get me," cried Dennis. "They'll creep
Under my monster bed, when I'm asleep."

"Oh, no," said his mummy, "I cannot agree,
There are no human beings, what fiddle-dee-fee.
They are only in stories. They do not exist.
Now get into bed and be quiet and kissed."

But when she bent down to kiss Dennis, he chose
To fasten his fangs round her warty old nose.
He tied up his toes in a knot round her knees.
"Led go of be, Deddid, you're hurtig be, please!"
"Only," he said, "if you help with my plan."
"All right," squealed his mummy, "I will if I can."

"Please take off my pillows and blankets," he said.
"From now on, I'd rather sleep under my bed,
For if I am there and a human comes near
It won't think to look for me, safe under here."

So there Dennis lay, staring up at the springs,
Thinking of birthdays and chocolate and things.

Now a certain small boy who played truant from school
Got lost in the wood, in the dark—little fool!

And feeling so tired he could wander no more
He stopped at the cave and he went through the door.
He saw the bare mattress, and desperate for rest
He peeled off his wellies and stripped to his vest.

He laid himself down and he shivered with fright.
He wished that his mummy could kiss him goodnight
And check that no monsters were under the bed.
But she wasn't there . . .

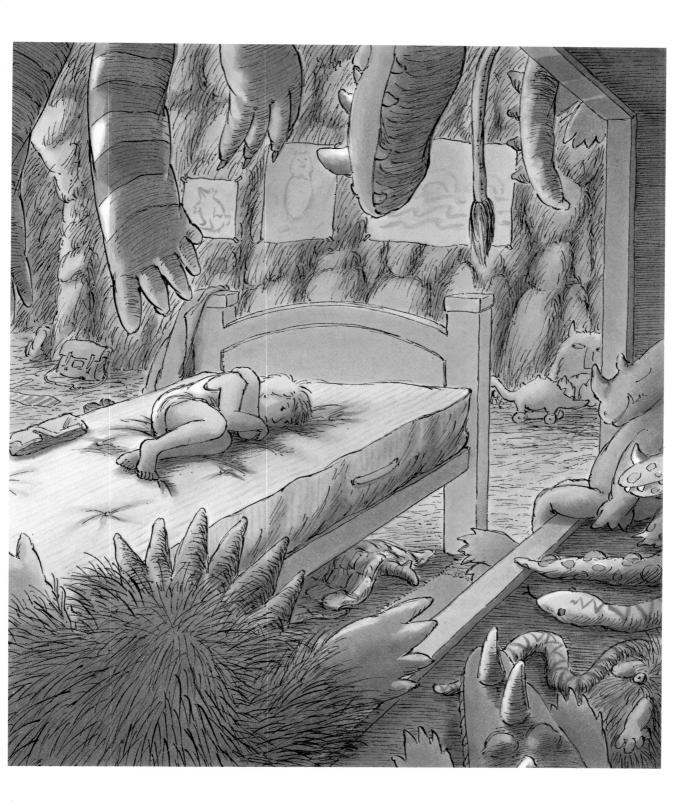

SO HE DID IT INSTEAD!

Other books by Jeanne Willis
(illustrated by Margaret Chamberlain)
The Tale of Georgie Grub
The Tale of Fearsome Fritz
The Tale of Mucky Mabel

Other books by Susan Varley
Badger's Parting Gifts
After Dark (written by Louis Baum)
The Fox and the Cat (written by Kevin Crossley-Holland)